Peggy –
Happy Valentine's Day 1979

Joel

Debbie's Dollhouse

Debbie's Dollhouse

A Story of Friendship, Fun and Imagination

Written by Barbara Kunz Loots
Illustrated by Pat Paris

Hallmark Children's Editions

DEBBIE'S DOLLHOUSE

Debbie Thompson climbed out of the camper and walked to the corner where a neighbor had said the school bus would stop. The day before, she and her parents had arrived at their new house. But the moving truck, packed with all their furniture from the old house a thousand miles away, was not there. So they spent the night parked in their own driveway.

Debbie waited for what seemed like a very long time. She leaned over the curb to see as far as she could down the street. What if this isn't the bus stop after all? she thought. What if I've already missed the bus? What if I'm late for school on my very first day?

Butterflies began to play ping-pong in her stomach. She glanced back toward the new house. Yesterday, she had stood in her empty bedroom, planning where the furniture should go. Would the huge, old dollhouse fit? The dollhouse was more than just a hobby. It was like a home where a part of Debbie herself really lived. She wouldn't feel comfortable until she knew the dollhouse was safe.

Debbie walked a little way up the sidewalk and back. What if something had happened to the moving truck? What if it didn't come at all? Debbie could just see all of their clothes and things flying out of the back of the truck as it rushed down the highway. And the dollhouse! What if something happened to the dollhouse?

No other children appeared. No bus arrived.

Just as the butterflies stopped playing games and started an all out war, Debbie heard a door slam somewhere down the block. Several children came dashing out to the sidewalk. At almost the same moment, the bus rumbled up to the corner and stopped.

Sitting way in the back, Debbie stared out the window, trying to look interested in the scenery. She imagined the funny looks she must be getting from the others. She tried not to care that nobody spoke to her. After all, what else could a new person expect?

At Barrett Elementary School, everyone piled out of the bus. Debbie found her way to the office. Mrs. Alexander, the principal, helped her enroll. After the first bell, she led Debbie through the quiet halls to the fifth grade. To the lions' den, thought Debbie.

"Class, this is Debbie Thompson. I hope you'll make her feel welcome," announced Mr. Graham, the teacher. "Amanda, will you please be Debbie's guide today, until she gets acquainted and knows her way around? She can sit behind you for the time being."

There was some scuffling and shuffling while the person in the desk behind Amanda was moved. Debbie stared at her feet, beginning to blush so deeply her face was almost shining.

Finally, somebody handed her a language arts book. It was the same book she had had in the old school. At once, the butterflies in her stomach began to settle down. Something, at least, was familiar! She glanced around. No lions in sight.

During morning recess, instead of going outside with the others, Amanda showed Debbie around the school. Debbie felt like a puppy dog trailing close at Amanda's heels, listening to Amanda talk and talk. Amanda seemed very self-assured.

"I hate gym, don't you?" said Amanda as they peeked into the little square windows in the gymnasium doors. Debbie liked gym, so she didn't mind not having a chance to answer as Amanda went right on talking.

After recess, the fifth grade filed into the art room to make mobiles. Debbie decided to make a tiny one to hang from the ceiling of the dollhouse nursery. The hour was over in a flash.

"I hate art, don't you?" said Amanda as they headed for the lunch-room together. Debbie just smiled. In one morning, she had learned that Amanda "hated" art, gym, music, crafts, older kids, riding bikes and homework. Debbie would have agreed with her on homework, at least. But Amanda never expected agreement, or disagreement, or even an-swers to most of her questions. So Debbie simply watched Amanda as she might watch someone on television putting on a performance.

"What do you like to do?" Debbie asked when Amanda stopped talk-ing long enough to eat her lunch.

"Oh, I don't know," Amanda mumbled through a mouthful. "Hang around, I guess. I mean, I'm not the type who has to be doing some-thing every minute, you know? I think everyone is entitled to do what they want, you know? I hope you're not one of those busy-busy types!"

"I guess not," said Debbie. "I spend most of my spare time working on the dollhouse."

"Dollhouse! Aren't you a little old to play dolls?"

Debbie explained that the dollhouse had belonged to her grand-mother in Maine where her family used to live. Debbie had helped make the furniture and decorations for the dollhouse. And when she moved away, her grandmother had given it to her.

"She called it an early heirloom," said Debbie. "But I'm worried it might get damaged in the move. It's pretty old."

Amanda yawned. "I hate Wednesdays, don't you?"

During the afternoon, Debbie paid close attention in order to mem-orize the names of everyone in the class. Amanda wasn't very good about introducing her to people, and by the time she climbed on the bus to go home, she had not spoken to a single other person in the class. Debbie decided to do something about that the second day, when she knew she wouldn't feel so lost.

As soon as she stepped off the bus, Debbie spotted the big moving truck outside her house.

"Hello! I'm home!" she yelled as she dashed through the front door, almost crashing into one of the movers coming out.

"Hello, Debbie!" Her father's voice rose, a little muffled, from behind a huge packing case in the living room. "You'd better go up to your room and have a close look at the dollhouse. I haven't had time, and the moving people will want to know everything's OK."

Debbie picked her way carefully through boxes and packing material scattered around the living room and darted up the stairs.

At the door of her bedroom, she stopped short. The dollhouse had already been unwrapped from its protective blankets. Standing on its low platform, it was taller than Debbie. She smiled, remembering the shape and color of every room even while the dollhouse was closed up. The afternoon sun shining into the dollhouse windows made lights and shadows inside as if it were a real house filled with life. It was Debbie's own friendly "home," no matter what house it happened to be sitting in, and she was glad to see it again.

Debbie walked around the dollhouse, checking the roof and walls for cracks and chips, and making sure the lacy metal decorations around the edge of the roof and the porch were not damaged. She noticed that one wall of the house had pulled away slightly from the other. Borrowing a hammer from the moving men, she carefully pounded it back in place. I'll need to reinforce it later, she thought.

She inspected all the crosspieces in the windows, which were without glass, and the golden glass strips on each side of the front door. Nothing was broken. And the little carved wooden eagle that spread its wings over the front door was still in place.

Then Debbie unhooked the fasteners on all sides, and carefully lifted away the whole front of the dollhouse. She unwound the electric cord tucked into one room, plugged it in, and switched on the lights. The white Christmas tree bulbs neatly installed out of sight in each room flashed on and filled every corner with light.

Debbie found a rag in a pile of cleaning supplies in the upstairs hall. She dusted the outside of the dollhouse, thinking that it could use a new coat of paint. Then she went to work on the inside.

It had been a long time since the dollhouse had been empty for a really good cleaning. The hallway and staircase, which divided the dollhouse into two sides, were the most difficult to clean, especially the intricately carved banisters.

On the bottom floor was the little bathroom with walls made of real ceramic tile. Fastened to the floor were a ceramic basin on a pedestal and an old-fashioned bathtub with feet like paws.

Beside the bathroom was the kitchen. Its black cast-iron stove came from a special store for dollhouses. Debbie had ordered the stove out of a catalog. She opened the tiny hinged door in its front. The tiny twigs cut into "logs" were still inside.

A little platform attached to a pulley travelled through a chute between the kitchen and the dining room on the floor just above, so that miniature residents could have dishes "hot" from the kitchen. Debbie

had designed this dumbwaiter and rigged it herself. At the top was a little bell on a spring that jangled every time the pulley was operated.

Across the hall from the dining room was the living room. It had a real marble fireplace with a fender around the front made of copper. Debbie had helped her grandmother paper the walls in red satin with velvet designs on it, which made the room look elegant even without any furniture in it.

On the third floor was the chinoiserie bedroom. Grandmother had called it that when they put in the flowered wallpaper that seemed oriental. Other furniture they made for this room looked oriental, too, almost like the furniture in some of the magazines they used for ideas.

The yellow nursery made up the rest of the third story. On one wall, Debbie had painted Humpty Dumpty sitting on his own brick wall. It looked the brightest and least empty of all the rooms, with its pretty calico curtains still hanging neatly at the windows.

At the very top of the house, in the cozy space under the slanting roof, was Debbie's favorite room. A little ladder extended from the third floor hall through a trapdoor into the attic. There was a tiny window seat in the alcove formed by the turret which jutted up in the front of the dollhouse. Sometimes, Debbie wished that she herself might curl up in this remote nook. Sitting beside the little round window at bird's-eye level, she could think about important things, and read, and dream. Maybe she'd be an interior designer when she grew up. Or an architect. Or an electrician. She had a lot of experience in those things — in miniature anyway. Or perhaps she might set up her very own dollhouse store.

Debbie and her parents ate a picnic supper in the middle of the half-unpacked things in the kitchen. Then they got to work together to un-pack enough lamps and linens and dishes to make their new house a little more comfortable. Debbie hoped to find the boxes containing her dollhouse furniture, too. Finally, she did.

"Oh, no! Look at this," she called out as she reached the bottom of the large carton of books she was unpacking. All the tiny furniture had been carefully wrapped in tissue and packed in its own separate box. Now, that box was flattened, or nearly so. Debbie couldn't hold back the tears as she fingered the broken bits of her little dining room set, the remains of the nursery chest of drawers and many other pieces of furniture from the dollhouse.

"The heavy books shifting must have done that," said her father, putting his arm around her shoulder.

"What a shame," her mother added. "You worked so hard making those things. That's too bad. But I'm sure some of them can be repaired.'' She tried to sound convincing, but Debbie wasn't hopeful as she inspected the broken pieces. After a few minutes, Debbie went back to the other unpacking.

Soon, she couldn't help feeling more cheerful. It was like a big Christmas with presents wrapped in newsprint. They discovered ''treasures'' they hardly remembered having had in the other house. And they found some funny things, too, like an old bologna sandwich, still wrapped in foil, that had been neatly packed with the kitchen things.

Debbie found another box containing some of the beautiful decorations that belonged in the dollhouse. There were two golden wall sconces made of dangling earrings from the dime store with tiny birthday candles in them. There was a matching chandelier that hung from a cup hook screwed in the ceiling of the dollhouse living room. There were some tiny pots and pans and potholders, and a little potted plant that usually sat on the windowsill in the dollhouse kitchen. And there were tiny boxes of ''ingredients'' and foods made from magazine pictures pasted to blocks of balsa wood cut the right size.

Debbie spent a few minutes looking at the little things and then took the whole box upstairs to her bedroom, where she put it away on the closet shelf. She wanted to have a lot of time to spend putting everything in its place in the dollhouse, and it had already been a long day.

At last, nearly everything was unpacked. The new Thompson house was beginning to look like home.

Very late, Debbie climbed into her old familiar bed and fell asleep, drifting into a dream that she was installing a huge wooden eagle over the door of a real house just like the dollhouse.

When Debbie left for the bus the second day, she felt like a different person from the day before. She actually smiled at the bus driver and sat down near the front. Several stops after Debbie's, one of the other girls in the fifth grade climbed on the bus.

"Hello," said Debbie, loudly enough to attract her attention. "You're Deena, aren't you?"

"How did you know my name?"

"Well, I spent the whole day in the same room with you yesterday," laughed Debbie. "We weren't exactly introduced, but I remember you because you've got pierced ears. My mom won't let me get my ears pierced yet. But I think yours look neat!" Deena sat right down next to Debbie and they talked about pierced ears for a while.

"You know, Debbie, when you spent the whole day yesterday with Amanda and nobody else, we decided you weren't very friendly. Besides, you sure did look stuck up when I saw you on the bus in the morning."

"Did I really look stuck up? Actually, I was pretty scared! And Amanda was helpful. But she spent so much time showing me around that she didn't give me a chance to meet anybody else."

"Well, Amanda doesn't really know anybody else very well. She went to private school before she came to Barrett at the beginning of the year. We tried to make friends with her, but all she talked about was her friends at the other school and all the things she used to do until the rest of us could hardly stand it. I guess we sort of started to ignore her, and she never seemed to care. She doesn't need us."

"I don't know," said Debbie. "Maybe somebody just needs to try a little harder to get to know her."

"Good luck."

When Debbie slid into her seat at school, Amanda turned around to visit. They talked until class began. Later, at recess, Amanda headed off toward a far corner of the playground.

"C'mon, Debbie. I've got my own private place where we can sit and talk," she called over her shoulder.

"Thanks, Amanda, but I promised Deena I'd play her a game of tetherball. Want to play with us?"

Amanda gave her a look that suggested Debbie had just crossed over to the other side in a kind of a war. "I hate tetherball. But go ahead. If that's what you want, it's all right with me."

Later on that morning, Mr. Graham asked Debbie to tell the class a little more about herself, and everyone listened politely while she talked about her parents and her old house and her new house.

Politeness changed to genuine interest when Debbie began to describe her special hobby. It was hard not to be interested in a dollhouse over three stories tall with everything on it, including electric lights and a doorbell!

"Unfortunately," Debbie concluded, "a lot of the furniture got squashed by accident when we moved, so now I have to start almost from scratch. It will take quite a while, but I have lots of ideas. I have to keep my eyes open to find things that could be used for the dollhouse."

"Find things like what?" asked a boy in the front.

"Well, for instance, one of the doorknobs looks like antique glass. Really it's a tiny crystal button off an old sweater. You know, the kind of button that makes colored sparkles. Every time I see an interesting button, I try to imagine what could be made with it. Everyone in my family and most of my friends have contributed something, or part of something, to the dollhouse, whether they meant to or not! I have several boxes filled with stuff I've found, just in case I might think of something to make out of it."

"What could you make out of this?" asked one of the girls, holding up the empty spool from a roll of cellophane tape. Debbie rolled the clear plastic cylinder around in her fingers for a moment. Then she described how a lamp could be made with it. Or a table.

"Here's a chest of drawers!" said someone else, digging into his pocket and producing an empty matchbox.

"That's perfect," said Debbie. "You can stack them up as high as you want, paint them or cover them with material, and add some knobs."

Debbie played this new "game" with several other objects that people held up. Soon, everyone was noisily examining and comparing bits and pieces they found in their desks, imagining and discussing what miniature gadgets or furnishings they might make out of them. Mr. Graham had to call the class to order.

"Now is a perfect time to make an important announcement. I can see how excited you are about Debbie's hobby. This ought to encourage you to think up one of your own, if you don't already have one. The P.T.A. is offering a prize of twenty-five dollars to the student presenting the best display of a hobby or special project in the school fair next month. We'll set aside a couple of hours each week for library research, or whatever kind of work you need to do on the project you select."

Going home, Deena wanted to hear more about the dollhouse.

"Why don't you come over and spend the night tomorrow?" said Debbie. "I'll check with my mom and call you later tonight."

"I'd like that! Talk to you later!" said Deena as the bus pulled up to her stop. Debbie waved good-bye out the window.

Deena brought her sleeping bag to school, with her pajamas and other things rolled up inside. As soon as the two girls arrived at Debbie's in the afternoon, they went to the dollhouse.

"Oh, Debbie, I've never seen anything like it! What a shame the furniture got broken."

"I have some plans," Debbie said. "I hope to have something made for every room by the time the hobby fair comes."

"Wouldn't it be great to have a real rocking horse in there?" said Deena, peeking through a window into the nursery. "One of my brother's plastic horses, painted, and put on some sort of rockers, would be just perfect."

"That's a good idea!" said Debbie. "Look, Deena. I know I can't finish this house by myself. At least, not in time for the fair. But with your help, we could win the prize. I'll split it with you fifty-fifty!"

"That's counting your chickens before they hatch!" laughed Deena. "But I'd love to help. This is the most fun hobby I ever heard of!"

After supper, Debbie and Deena got out the "junk boxes." In the various containers, appropriately labelled, were bits of lace, printed cotton, taffeta, velvet and damask; hairpins and straight pins; spools of various sizes; pieces of foam, styrofoam and balsa wood; pictures cut from magazines, gift wrap and wallpaper scraps; cardboard patterns for furniture; pieces of old jewelry, and other odds and ends. A large box contained Debbie's work tools: glue, scissors, a measuring tape, a ruler, graph paper, tweezers, a small saw and some paintbrushes. There were also stacks of books and magazines that Debbie and her grandmother had used for ideas.

The two girls sorted through junk and scribbled ideas on paper until long after Debbie's parents were asleep. Then they tiptoed downstairs for a midnight snack of peanut butter on a spoon.

Monday morning, Debbie decided to try all over again to make friends with Amanda.

"Have you decided on your project yet, Amanda?"

"Well, I had an ant farm," answered Amanda. "But all the ants died."

"Oh. That's too bad." Debbie couldn't think of anything else to say. Somehow Amanda's ant farm didn't sound too exciting. But Debbie was determined to keep the conversation going at least until the bell rang.

"Amanda, I've been riding my bike around to get to know the neighborhood. Can I ride over to your house sometime?"

"I guess it's not too far," said Amanda, taking out a pencil to write down the address. "You can come over Saturday morning if you want."

When Debbie arrived the next Saturday, Amanda's brother answered the door. He pointed to the family room and ran out. Debbie found Amanda stretched out in front of the television. I guess this is what she meant by "hanging around," thought Debbie. Amanda said hello and shoved another floor cushion at Debbie.

After they had been watching television for quite a while without even talking to each other, Debbie began to wonder if the long ride to Amanda's, just to be friendly, was worth the trouble. She almost invited Amanda to go bike riding with her, but then she remembered Amanda hated bikes. Finally, when a commercial came on, and Debbie was tired of sitting still, she asked Amanda whether or not she had thought of another project for the hobby fair.

"Oh, I don't care about that," said Amanda. "It's too much bother."

"Amanda, the trouble with you is, you never want to bother about anything!" said Debbie, a little louder than she intended. "You just hate everything. All you want to do is watch the dumb old TV!"

Amanda whirled around, her expression transformed in a second from boredom to anger.

"Who asked you, Miss Priss? What I want to do is my own business, and who my friends are, too, so you can just get out of here and go play with your dumb dollhouse! I hate you!"

Debbie stiffened at the words. She felt the prickle in her nose that tears make when they're about to surface, and the red flush began to creep up her neck, not from anger but from shame.

"I'm sorry, Amanda. I shouldn't have said that. It isn't really true. You did bother about me that first day when I was new. And scared."

"You didn't act scared," said Amanda cooly. "And right away you joined up with those other girls. I'll bet they had plenty of mean things to tell you about me!"

"No, they didn't," said Debbie. "They thought you had lots of other friends from your old school, that's all, and that you didn't need them. But I wanted to know you better, and that's why I came over today. But I guess I've spoiled everything now, so I'll just go home."

"Wait a minute, Debbie. Wait. Look, I don't really hate you. I say that all the time. Why don't we just start over at nothing to nothing."

Debbie and Amanda shared a root beer and talked about school, especially about being "the new person." Debbie was expecting Deena over to work on the dollhouse in the afternoon, and she invited Amanda to come back home with her. "I know you don't care much for dolls and stuff, but it will give you a chance to get to know Deena a little better. If you want to, that is."

"Might as well," said Amanda. "Most of the programs on Saturday afternoon are reruns anyway."

"I don't believe it!" exclaimed Amanda the moment she saw the dollhouse. "When you talked about it, I never imagined anything like this! It's like something I saw on TV one time, in a museum!"

Amanda was still on her knees peering into the dollhouse and asking questions about all the things that were in it when Deena arrived. Debbie could see how surprised Deena was to find Amanda there, and even more surprised that Amanda was so interested in the dollhouse.

"Amanda's ants died, so I invited her over to have a look at the dollhouse. Now she'd like to help us get the dollhouse ready for the hobby fair. Do you mind?"

"Well, I guess not," said Deena with a puzzled look at Amanda.

The three girls were soon deeply involved in dollhouse plans. They talked about what would be needed for each room. Amanda came up with some clever new ideas when she looked at the things in the junk boxes. And by the end of the afternoon, Amanda and Deena, laughing and talking as if they had known each other all their lives, began to wonder how they could have missed making friends long before.

After that first afternoon, Debbie, Deena and Amanda spent most of their spare time together working on the dollhouse. They weren't always at Debbie's house. Mr. Zimmerman at the hardware store knew all three by name before long. So did the people who owned the fabric store and the hobby store at the shopping center. The store people didn't mind donating scraps of things to the dollhouse, and the three girls spent some of their allowances to buy supplies. They also ordered from Debbie's catalogs some special furniture and fixtures they couldn't make.

Word about the dollhouse spread around school. People they didn't even know stopped Debbie or Deena or Amanda on the playground to give them an interesting looking button or a miniature toy from a gum ball machine or little empty boxes and bottles that medicines came in. They almost always asked, "What can you do with this?"

One afternoon, close to the time for the hobby fair, Debbie was putting the finishing touches on the dollhouse bathroom. Carefully, she tapped a tiny nail into the wall near the ceiling. From it, on a gold cord, she hung a little curved mirror. When a person looked into the bathroom, she would see herself reflected in miniature.

"Hey, I just had a fantastic idea!" Debbie shouted out loud. Amanda and Deena, who were concentrating on their own projects, nearly jumped out of their chairs. "Why don't we put in running water!"

"That's impossible!" said Amanda. "It's too small!"

"Where would you get the water without moving the whole dollhouse into the kitchen or something?" Deena added.

"I don't know yet," said Debbie, fingering the tiny bathroom fixtures. "But I want to try it. Just think how surprised everyone would be at the hobby fair!"

"They'll be pretty impressed as it is, if you ask me!" said Amanda. But Debbie's friends went along with her to Mr. Zimmerman's hardware store to poke around and see what kinds of things could be used to put plumbing in a dollhouse.

The day of the hobby fair brought perfect spring weather. The girls helped load the dollhouse into Deena's father's pick-up truck. Then they climbed in beside it with four boxes of little furniture and tiny accessories which they had removed from the house. Holding on carefully to their precious cargo, they arrived safely at the school.

The playground on this Saturday was busier than most school days. It looked as if everyone in town were at recess. There were kids from all the grades and kids from other schools. There were brothers and sisters and parents and grandparents and relatives and friends. There was even a reporter from the local television station with a camera crew.

Deena's father drove the truck as close as possible to the spot that had been assigned for the hobby exhibits. They unloaded the dollhouse and positioned it carefully on its platform. Even outdoors, it looked enormous. Quite a few people gathered around as the three girls unpacked the furniture and returned everything to its proper place in the dollhouse. Last of all, they set up a neatly printed sign right in front.

Projects and hobbies were lined up along the edge of the asphalt playground. Each student stood nearby to explain his or her project. There were stamp collections, coin collections and butterfly collections. There were models of all kinds: airplanes, cars, trains and ships. One girl displayed a model skyscraper "under construction," complete with a motorized elevator. Two boys displayed signal flags they had designed and made to send messages out the windows between their houses. Some of the junior high boys brought the things they had learned to bake or sew in a new class called "Bachelor Survival."

Everyone stopped to admire the dollhouse. The girls removed some of the tinier objects so they could be looked at more closely. People were surprised to find tiny socks tucked into the dresser drawers and folded napkins neatly laid in the dining room cupboard. There were real wicks in the tops of the tiny candles on the mantel in the living room. There were even crumbles of "dog food" in the puppy's dish.

The most surprised people of all were the other fifth graders. They had been in on the project from the beginning more than anybody else, even though they hadn't ever seen the dollhouse.

"Hey, that's my old broken watch!" exclaimed Tom. Except Tom's watch face had been transformed into part of a real grandfather clock standing in the hallway. Elizabeth's broken locket had become a tiny picture frame. And the tops from Chuck's used oil paint tubes, stacked up and glued together, were lamps topped with stylish fluted shades.

Finally, the judges for the hobby fair arrived at the dollhouse. Debbie, Deena and Amanda stood to one side as each of the three judges examined it, asking questions and holding up the tiny furniture to admire the workmanship.

When the judges appeared to be done, Debbie stepped forward and spoke up in a voice that sounded a lot like Mr. Graham's when he made his important announcements.

"We would like to present a special demonstration!" She reached into the dollhouse and turned a little handle on the spigot in the kitchen sink. Real water began to flow from the faucet in a delicate, dollhouse-sized trickle. Debbie turned another little knob in the bathtub, and water ran out of that spigot also. When the basins were filled, Debbie turned the water off. Jiggling in tiny pools, the water made the dollhouse look more real than ever.

Debbie showed the judges the jar that was the storage tank fastened under the eaves of the house. Two thin plastic tubes came out of the rubber stopper in the jar, one leading into the dollhouse bathroom, the other into the kitchen. Debbie had designed a tiny pinching mechanism at each faucet to control the flow of water and had painted the end of each tube silver to look like metal.

The judges nodded thoughtfully and smiled at one another. They thanked the three girls for their demonstration and moved on to the next display. Soon, just about everyone on the playground had heard about the new feature in the dollhouse and stopped by to see it work. The three dollhouse designers took turns running to fill up the little water storage tank to keep the supply going.

Before the end of the afternoon, Debbie's Dollhouse had a new decoration: a bright blue ribbon with three streamers waving from its rooftop. As the television cameras whirred, the judges presented the prize check to all three girls to be divided equally among them.

At news time that evening, Debbie, Deena and Amanda sat on top of their sleeping bags spread out in Debbie's family room. The headline appeared on the screen:

PINT-SIZED PLUMBERS WIN PRIZE

"There we are! There we are! We're on television!" screeched Amanda joyously. And all three girls grinned at each other, just like they were grinning on the screen while the judges presented the prize.

"What are you going to do with your share of the money, Amanda?" asked Deena.

"Oh, I was thinking of investing in an ant farm!" All three girls burst out laughing.

"I'm going to start building a dollhouse of my own," said Deena. "Maybe just one room at a time."

"That's a good idea!" said Amanda. "Hey, maybe we could each make a room the same size and eventually put them together into the biggest dollhouse ever!"

Debbie smiled at both of her friends.

"Don't you think you're a little old to play dolls?" she said, giving Amanda a teasing poke.